HOPSCO[tch]
the Tiny bunny

Written by Stephanie Calmenson
Illustrated by Barbara Lanza

A GOLDEN BOOK • NEW YORK
Western Publishing Company, Inc., Racine, Wisconsin 53404

Mr. and Mrs. Rabbit had a house full of bunnies. That made them very proud.

One morning Mr. Rabbit asked his bunnies to line up so he could count them.

"One, two, three, four, five..."

He counted up to ten.

"Wait!" cried Hopscotch, the tiny bunny at the center of the line.

Hopscotch ran to his father and hopped up, up, up to his father's shoulder.

"Oooh, that tickles!" Mr. Rabbit said with a laugh.

"You forgot to count *me*!" Hopscotch shouted in his father's ear.

"I am so sorry," said Mr. Rabbit. "I will not let it happen again." He gave Hopscotch a big hug.

That night Mrs. Rabbit was cutting carrot pie for her bunnies' dessert. "One, two, three, four, five…"

She counted up to ten. Then she cut one piece for herself and one for Mr. Rabbit.

"Wait!" cried Hopscotch. "You forgot to cut a piece of pie for *me*!"

"I am so sorry," said Mrs. Rabbit. She gave Hopscotch the piece of pie she had cut for herself. And she let him sit on her lap while he ate it.

When he finished eating his pie, Hopscotch
went outside to join his sisters and brothers. They
decided to play hide-and-seek.

"Ready or not, here I come!" called his brother.

Hopscotch hid behind a mushroom, waiting to be
found. He waited a very long time. He was still waiting
when the sun went down. He was still waiting when he
fell fast asleep.

The next morning Hopscotch woke all alone and a little confused. He started for home, but turned the wrong way. He hopped and hopped and hopped.

The world looks very big to a bunny as tiny as Hopscotch. Blades of grass seem as tall as trees. Rocks become mountains. And a cat is as big as...

"Meowwww!" screeched the cat.

"Run for your life!" called a voice.

Hopscotch followed the voice down into a hole in the ground.
"Meowww!" screeched the cat angrily.
"You're safe now," said a small gray field mouse.
"Thank you," said Hopscotch.
The mouse looked closely at Hopscotch.

"You're small, but you're not a mouse, are you? Your ears are long, and your tail is short and round. You look like a rabbit to me," said the mouse.

"I *am* a rabbit," said Hopscotch.

"Whatever you are, you're just the right size," said the mouse. "My name is Squeak. Do you want to play?"

"Sure!" said Hopscotch.

They peeked out. The cat was nowhere in sight.

"Let's play hide-and-seek!" said Squeak. "You hide first."

Hopscotch was a little nervous about playing. But he agreed.

"Ready or not, here I come!" called Squeak.

Hopscotch waited. And waited. Then Squeak called, "I found you!"

"How did you find me so fast?" asked Hopscotch.

"I never saw a mushroom with long, fuzzy ears before!" Squeak said, laughing.

Hopscotch got to choose next. "Let's have a race!" he said.
They were just the same speed.

They skipped rope.

They had a catch.

They could even play leapfrog because they were just the same size.

Hopscotch and Squeak played until they were tired and very hungry. They picked some leaves and seeds and went to the stream for a picnic.

While they were eating, Hopscotch told Squeak how he got lost. "My family always forgets me. They probably don't even know I'm gone now."

"My family forgets me, too," said Squeak. "That's why I wrote them a note and ran away."

The two friends sat quietly, eating and thinking.

Finally Squeak said, "I miss my family."

"I miss mine, too," said Hopscotch. "Let's go find them."

Back at the Rabbit house, Mr. and Mrs. Rabbit and ten bunnies were worried sick.

Mr. Rabbit had lined up his bunnies. This time he called, "Hopscotch! You're the number one bunny today!" But Hopscotch did not answer. Mr. Rabbit called him again. Still no answer.

The Rabbits looked high and low for Hopscotch. His brothers and sisters hoped he was just playing.

"Come out, come out, wherever you are!" they called.

But Hopscotch did not come out. Finally Mrs. Rabbit cried, "Hopscotch is really gone!"

The Rabbits set out to find him.

"Let's stick together," said Mr. Rabbit. "We don't want to lose any more of our bunnies."

At the same time, the Mouse family was out looking for Squeak.

Sniff. Sniff. There was a strong smell in the air. It smelled like...

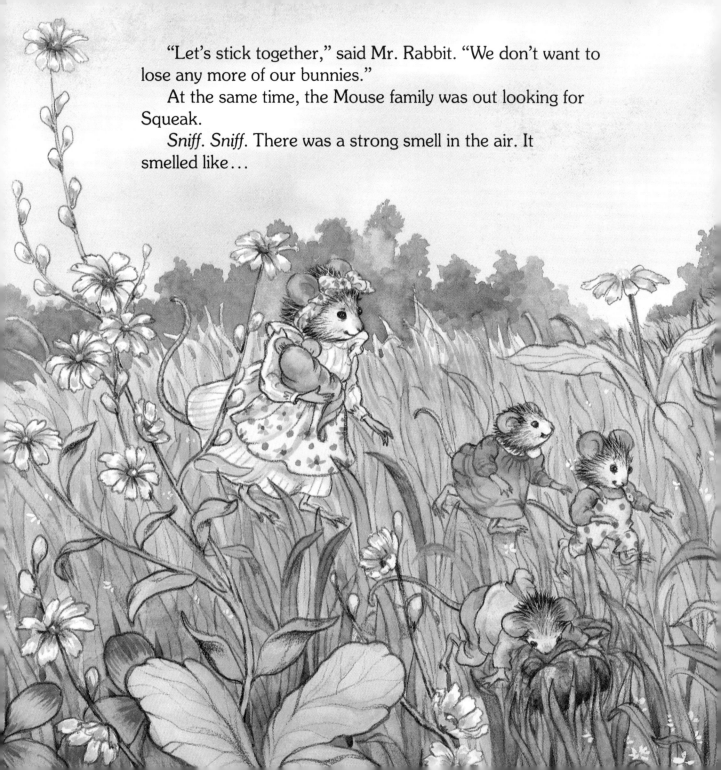

"*Meowww!*" screeched the big fat cat.
Mr. and Mrs. Rabbit and their bunnies ran *this* way.
Mr. and Mrs. Mouse and their mice ran *that* way.
Hopscotch and Squeak headed for their hole in the
ground and…

They all ended up in the same place—
rabbits and mice all mixed up together.

"Mommy! Mommy! Daddy! Daddy!"

"Hopscotch!"

"Squeak!"

The cat did not make a sound. He was scared. He had
never seen so many rabbits and mice all in one place before.
He turned around and ran away.

After much hugging and kissing, Hopscotch and Squeak told their families everything that had happened.

They all got along so well that the Mouse family moved in next door to the Rabbits.

Every morning Mr. Rabbit counted eleven bunnies to make sure they were all there.

Every night Mr. Mouse counted eight mice.

Hopscotch and Squeak stayed best friends.
And no one ever forgot either one of them again.